ZIGBY ™
CAMPS OUT

BRIAN PATERSON

HarperCollins*Publishers*

For William, Charles, and Henry

Zigby Camps Out
Text copyright © 2002 by Alan MacDonald, Brian Paterson, and
HarperCollins Publishers Ltd.
Illustrations copyright © 2002 by Brian Paterson
Printed in Belgium. All rights reserved.
www.harperchildrens.com
First published in the United Kingdom by HarperCollins Publishers Ltd., 2002
First U.S. edition, 2003
Library of Congress Cataloging-in-Publication Data
Paterson, Brian.
Zigby camps out / Brian Paterson.—1st U.S. ed.
p.   cm.
Summary: When Zigby the zebra receives a new tent, he and his friends Bertie Bird and
McMeer go camping in the deepest jungle.
ISBN 0-06-052921-0
[1. Zebras—Fiction.   2. Camping—Fiction.   3. Jungle animals—Fiction.]   I. Title.
PZ7.P27245 Zi   2003   [E]—dc21   2002008874
1 2 3 4 5 6 7 8 9 10
❖

Follow the winding stream to the edge of the jungle
and meet...

ZIGBY
THE ZEBRA
OF MUDWATER CREEK.

Zigby loves exploring new places and playing
with his friends, Bertie Bird and McMeer.
Sometimes, though, he can't help
trotting straight into trouble!

Bertie Bird is an African guinea fowl.
He's easily scared—but he'd hate to miss his
friends' adventures!

McMeer the meerkat is a show-off
and a prankster who always knows how
to have fun!

HIGH ABOVE MUDWATER CREEK,
ZIGBY LIVES IN HIS TREE HOUSE.
One morning Zigby received a
strange package from his aunt Zandra.
He ripped it open.
"Just what I always wanted!" he shouted.
He hurried to show his friends.

McMeer sniffed the lumpy shape.
"Is it a sausage?" he asked hopefully.

"Don't be silly." Zigby laughed.
"It's a tent. Let's go camping!"

McMeer rolled head over heels. He'd never been camping before. Neither had Bertie, who hoped it wasn't too dangerous.

The friends set out.

Zigby grabbed a swishy stick in case they ran into anything scary.

"Where are you going?" asked Ella the elephant.

"We're going to camp in the darkest jungle," said Zigby.

"Better take a watermelon," said Ella.

"Camping is hungry work."

"Let's go!" said Zigby.

They climbed
tall mountains…

waded across
swamps…

…and fought through tangled forests.

Finally, Zigby said,
"Stop! This is it—
the darkest
jungle."

Putting up the tent was tricky.
There were so many poles and pegs!
"It's a bit crooked, but it will do,"
said McMeer.

They squashed inside.

"This is fun!" said Zigby.

"When do we eat?" asked Bertie.

"First we need a fire," said McMeer.

"I'll get some wood."

Zigby and Bertie waited in the tent.
The sun set and the jungle grew dark.
Bertie moved closer to Zigby.
"What's that noise?" he whispered.
"What noise?" asked Zigby.
"That something-lurking-in-the-dark noise," said Bertie.
Zigby listened and he heard it, too.
He reached for his swishy stick.

Bertie moved even closer to Zigby.
"What's *that* noise?" he whispered.
"What noise?" asked Zigby.

"That something-waiting-to-pounce noise," said Bertie.
Zigby listened and he heard it, too…a rustling,
scuffling sound…coming closer.

Bertie clung to Zigby.
"It's right outside!" he cried.
"I can hear it dribbling and snarling."
"I hear it, too," said Zigby, "and

THERE IT IS!"

A tall shadow loomed
over them. Bravely, Zigby
poked through the tent
with his swishy stick.

"Ow!"
said a voice.

"It's McMeer!" cried Zigby.
"And he's eating the last of the watermelon!" said Bertie.
"Did I scare you?" McMeer giggled.

Zigby and Bertie made McMeer
build the fire by himself.
"And you're not coming in
until it's finished," said Zigby.

As McMeer put the last log on the fire,
he heard a sound like distant thunder.
He pricked up his ears.

It was coming toward them...

…growing louder and

LOUDER.

The ground shook and the trees trembled.

McMeer grabbed the tent.

"Let me in!" he begged. "Something's coming!"

"McMeer, stop playing games," answered Zigby.

"Don't leave me out here. Please!" wailed McMeer.
Zigby and Bertie listened. They heard the noise, too.
Bertie opened the tent flap and McMeer dived inside.
The friends huddled together in the dark.

"THUMP!

 THUMP!

THUMP!"

Suddenly something long and snakelike
reached into the tent…

It was Ella! "Hello!" she said.
"I came to say good night. Are you having a good time?"
"No! We're cold and hungry," said Bertie,
"and McMeer ate all the watermelon."
"Well, why don't you come home?"
asked Ella. "I've made supper."

After the best supper ever,
everyone was ready for bed.
"What about your tent?" asked Ella.
"I know just the place for it," said Zigby.

Good night, Zigby.